The Bunny That Couldn't Hop

Annie Miller

ISBN: 1497435188
ISBN-13: 978-1497435186

Dedicated to my honey bunnies ~ Jon, Katie Scarlett, and Michael

One day in the forest not too long ago, there lived a little mother bunny. She had three baby bunnies, two girls and one boy.

The mother bunny named the girls Cotton and Marshmallow.
The boy, who was slightly smaller, she named Raisins.

The bunnies grew and grew. Soon it was time to take them out for a walk. Mother Bunny said, "Put on your mittens," and off they went.

Marshmallow and Cotton hopped around every tree and bush playing, but Raisins couldn't hop. No matter how hard he tried, he just couldn't do it.

Finally, Mother Bunny said, "It's getting late. Time to go home for dinner."

At **dinner**, Marshmallow and Cotton talked about all the fun they had hopping through the forest, but Raisins just ate sadly.

One morning, Raisins heard his mother and another mother bunny talking. The other mother said, "As you know, my little Fluffy couldn't twitch her nose. We took her to the Great Bunny, and ever since, she has been twitching perfectly."

"Who is the Great Bunny?" Raisins wondered. "Can he help me hop?"

After lunch, Raisins got permission from his mother and set out to find the Great Bunny. Soon he came to a fork in the road and didn't know which way to go.

Raisins looked around and spotted an owl. "Hello wise Owl. Can you please tell me how to get to the Great Bunny's house?" he asked.

"Why you're on your way right now," said the owl. "Go left at the fork and turn right at the berry patch. Then follow the wire fence all the way to the red brick walk that leads straight to his door. You can't miss it."

"Thank you!" Raisins called as he began the walk that
he hoped would change his life.

Raisins followed along just as the owl said and soon found himself beneath a huge oak door.

Now afraid, Raisins wondered if he should be there at all. But his aching feet reminded him how tiring the long **walk** had been, and the thought of hopping gave him the courage to reach up and knock.

Knock, knock, knock.

The door opened to such a friendly face that Raisins was no longer afraid. "Are you the Great Bunny?" Raisins asked.

"Yes, how may I help you?"

"My name is Raisins, and more than anything, I want to hop."

"I see," said the Great Bunny. "Come in and we'll talk."

Raisins explained his problem, and the Great Bunny replied, "Only you can make yourself hop. You just have to keep trying. Don't give up. But trust me, soon you will be the best hopper in the forest."

Raisins left disappointed.

It was getting late, so Raisins decided to take a shortcut home. He knew that he would have to cross the old bridge, but he had to be home before dark.

When Raisins got there, the bridge was out!
"Oh no!" He thought. "Now what will I do?"

Just then Raisins heard a noise behind him in the woods. It was a hungry wolf! He had to get away! But how? He couldn't **walk** across the rushing water below. All at once Raisins knew what he had to do.

Twitching nervously, he curled up into a tight little ball...

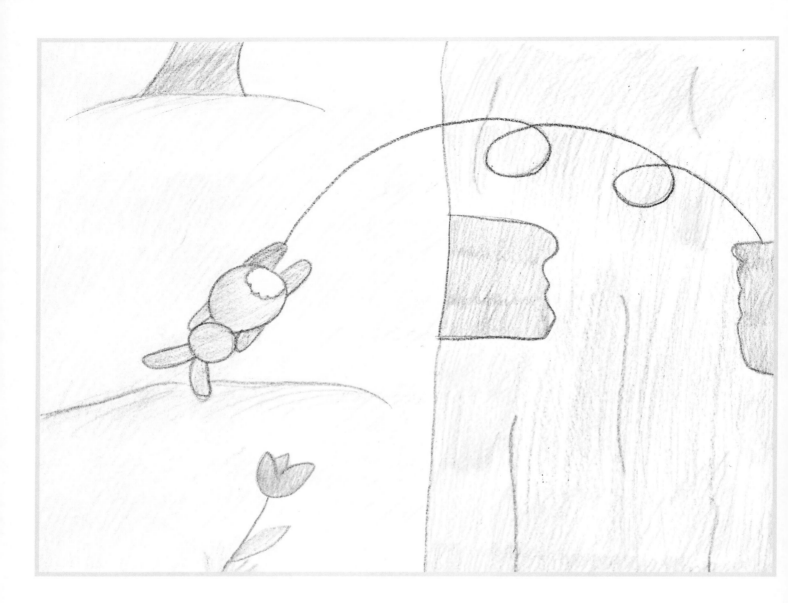

All it took was one more howl from that hungry wolf, and Raisins pushed off with all his might. He flew through the air and landed safely on the other side of the stream.

He did it! He hopped!

The wolf couldn't get him now.

26

Raisins was so proud of himself that he hopped happily all the way home.

And from that day on, he truly was …

the
  best
    hopper
      in the
        forest.

About the Author

Annie Miller wrote <u>The Bunny That Couldn't Hop</u> in 1988 for a sixth grade English project when she attended Our Lady of Peace elementary school in Canton, Ohio. She carefully drew and colored the pictures and received an A++ from her teacher, Mrs. Sandy Risaliti. Annie treasured the book and kept it safe for years until it was time to read it to her own children. They loved the book so much that she decided to publish it for other children to enjoy. This book contains the original text and drawings that Annie made in sixth grade.

Annie went on to earn her Ph.D. in biochemistry from The Ohio State University and is now a stay-at-home mom with three children.

4426064R00022

Printed in Germany
by Amazon Distribution
GmbH, Leipzig